CU00252880

MINI CLASSICS

ALI BABA
AND THE
FORTY THIEVES

A Parragon Book

Published by
Parragon Books,
Unit 13–17, Avonbridge Trading Estate,
Atlantic Road, Avonmouth, Bristol BS11 9QD.

Produced by
The Templar Company plc,
Pippbrook Mill, London Road, Dorking, Surrey RH4 1JE.

Designed by Mark Kingsley-Monks

Printed and bound in Great Britain

ISBN 1-85813-655-5

MINI CLASSICS

ALI BABA
AND THE
FORTY THIEVES

RETOLD BY STEPHANIE LASLETT
ILLUSTRATED BY HELEN COCKBURN

In a town in Persia there lived two brothers, one named Cassim, the other Ali Baba.

Cassim was married to a rich wife and lived in a fine house with plenty to eat and drink. His brother, Ali Baba, was very poor and looked after his wife and children by cutting wood in a nearby forest and selling it in the town.

One day, when Ali Baba was working in the forest, he saw a troop of men on horseback coming towards him in a cloud of dust. He was afraid they were robbers and climbed into a tree for safety.

Soon they were passing beneath him and, to his surprise, they pulled up their horses and dismounted. Ali Baba counted forty men.

The finest man among them, whom Ali Baba took to be their Captain, went a little way among some bushes, and said "Open, Sesame!" so clearly that Ali Baba heard him.

A door in the rocks swung slowly open, and the Captain ordered his troop of men to go in. Then he followed and the door closed behind them.

They stayed inside some time and Ali Baba, fearing they might come out and catch him, was forced to sit patiently in the tree.

At last the door opened again. The Captain came out, and watched carefully as his Forty Thieves passed by him. Then he closed the door, saying "Shut, Sesame!" Each man mounted his horse and off they galloped into the distance with a great thundering of hooves.

Then Ali Baba climbed down and went to the secret door hidden behind the bushes. "Open, Sesame!" he cried, and the door flew open. Ali Baba expected to see a dark, dismal hole but he was greatly surprised to find a large cave with a hole in the roof to let the light in.

The cave was full of treasure. Before him lay great heaps of silver and gold, carpets of velvet and silk and bags overflowing with coins.

13

Ali Baba entered the cave and the door shut behind him. He went straight for the gold and picked up as many bags as he thought his asses could carry.

Quickly he loaded his animals with the gold, and then hid the treasure beneath bundles of sticks.

"Shut, Sesame!" said Ali Baba. The door closed and he went home.

Ali Baba drove his asses into the yard, shut the gates and carried the money bags to his wife.

"We must keep this secret," he told her. "I will bury the gold in the garden."

"First let me measure it," said his wife. "I will borrow a measuring jar from someone while you dig the hole."

So she ran to the wife of

Cassim and borrowed a measuring jar. Knowing Ali Baba was poor, Cassim's wife was curious to find out what sort of grain Ali Baba wished to measure, and so she put some lard in the bottom of the jar.

Ali Baba's wife went home and measured the gold. Over and over again she filled, then emptied the jar. How happy she was!

But when she returned the jar, she did not notice that a piece of gold was stuck to the lard in the bottom.

As soon as she had left, Cassim's wife spotted the gold and she grew very curious. When Cassim came home she said:

"Cassim, your brother is richer than you. He does not count his money — he *measures* it."

19

He begged her to explain this riddle, which she did by showing him the piece of money and telling him where she found it. Then Cassim grew so envious that he could not sleep.

Before sunrise next morning he visited his brother. "Ali Baba," he said, showing him the gold piece, "you pretend to be poor and yet you are measuring gold." Ali Baba realised that thanks to his wife's foolishness, Cassim and his wife had discovered their secret. Straightaway he confessed what he had done and offered Cassim a share of the money.

"Of course I shall have a share," said Cassim, angrily, "but I must know where the treasure is hidden, or there will be trouble!"

Ali Baba, more out of
kindness than fear, told
him about the cave, and
the exact words to use.

So Cassim left Ali Baba.
He intended to cheat him
and get all the treasure for
himself. He rose early next
morning and set out with
ten mules loaded with great
chests. He soon found the
place, and the secret door
in the rock.

"Open, Sesame!" he cried
and the door opened and
shut behind him. He could
have feasted his eyes all
day on the treasures, but
quickly he began to gather
together as much as he
could carry.

But when he was ready to go he was so busy thinking about his great riches that he could not remember what to say. Instead of "Sesame," he said "Open, Barley!" and the door remained fast. He named several different sorts of grain, all but the right one, and the door still stuck fast. He was so frightened of the danger he was in that the word went right out of his head.

About noon the robbers returned to their cave, and saw Cassim's mules roving about with great chests on their backs. Someone was stealing their treasure!

Quickly they drew their sabres and surrounded the cave. "Open, Sesame!" cried the Captain and the door swung open.

Cassim heard the trampling of their horses' feet and was determined not to die without a fight, so when the door opened he jumped out and threw the Captain down. In vain, however, for the robbers with their sabres soon killed him.

Then the thieves saw Cassim's bags laid ready, and they could not imagine how anyone had got in without knowing their secret. They cut Cassim's body into four quarters, and nailed them up inside the cave, in order to frighten anyone else who might venture inside, then off they went in search of more treasure.

As night drew on Cassim's wife grew very anxious. She ran to her brother-in-law, and told him where her husband had gone.

Ali Baba comforted her and then set out for the forest with his asses in search of Cassim. The first thing he saw on entering the cave was his dead brother.

Full of horror, he laid the body on one of his asses, and the bags of gold on the other two and, covering everything with bundles of sticks, he returned home.

He drove the asses laden with gold into his own yard, and led the other to Cassim's house. The door was opened by the slave Morgiana, whom he knew to be brave and cunning.

Unloading the ass, he said to her, "This is the body of your master. He has been murdered, but we must bury him as though he had died peacefully in his bed. I will speak with you again, but now go and tell your mistress that I have arrived."

When Cassim's wife heard the terrible news of her husband's death, she began to wail and cry. So Ali Baba offered to take her to live with him and his wife.

"But you must promise to follow my advice and leave everything to Morgiana," he said. Gladly Cassim's wife agreed, and she dried her eyes.

Meanwhile, Morgiana had

thought of a plan. She visited an apothecary and bought some pills. "My poor master can neither eat nor speak," she said, "and no-one knows what ails him." She returned home with the pills, but went back the next day.

"He is worse," she wept. "I need the strongest medicine you have, for I fear that he will die."

That evening no-one was
surprised to hear the
wretched shrieks and cries
of Cassim's wife and
Morgiana, telling everyone
that Cassim was dead.

Early the next day,
Morgiana went to an old
cobbler near the gates of
the town. She put a piece
of gold in his hand, and
told him she had some
work for him to do.

She blindfolded him with a scarf, then led him to the room where Cassim's body lay. She removed the old man's blindfold and asked him to sew the four quarters together. The poor cobbler did as he was told and then, with his eyes covered, he was led back to his home.

Then they buried Cassim, and Morgiana followed him to the grave, weeping and tearing her hair, while Cassim's wife stayed at home and wept bitter tears. Next day she went to live with Ali Baba, who gave Cassim's shop to his eldest son.

When the Forty Thieves returned to the cave, they were astonished to find that Cassim's body had gone and yet more of their moneybags were missing.

"We are certainly discovered," said the Captain, "and shall be undone if we cannot find out who it is that knows our secret. Two men must have known it; we have killed one, we must now find the other.

"I need one bold and cunning robber to go into the city dressed as a traveller and discover whom we have killed, and

whether there is talk about the manner of his death. If this messenger fails he must lose his life, for we could all be betrayed by him."

One of the thieves jumped up and offered to do it, and, as the other robbers praised him for his bravery, he disguised himself.

At daybreak he entered the town, close by the stall of Baba Mustapha, the cobbler. The thief wished him good-day, saying,

"Old man, how can you possibly see to stitch at your great age?"

47

"Old as I am," replied the cobbler, "I have very good eyes. Believe me when I tell you that only recently I sewed a dead body together in a place where I had less light than I have now."

The robber was overjoyed at his good fortune and, giving the cobbler a piece of gold, asked to be shown the house where he had stitched up the dead body.

At first Mustapha refused, saying that he had been blindfolded, but when the robber gave him another piece of gold he began to think he might remember the way if he was blindfolded just as before.

The plan succeeded, for the robber partly led the cobbler, and was partly guided by him, right to the front of Cassim's house.

The robber marked the door with a piece of chalk. Then, well pleased, he said farewell to Baba Mustapha and returned to the forest.

51

By-and-by Morgiana saw
the mark the robber had
made, and quickly guessed
that some mischief was
brewing. She fetched a piece
of chalk and marked two
or three doors along the
street with a similar cross,
without saying anything to
her master or mistress.

The thief, meantime, was
busy telling the other
robbers of his discovery.

The Captain thanked him, and wanted to see the house he had marked. But when they came to it, they saw that five or six other houses were chalked in the same manner.

The robber was so confused that he was lost for words, and when they returned he was at once beheaded for having failed. Another robber was sent off and, having once again bribed Baba Mustapha to show him the way, he marked the door with red chalk, but Morgiana was still too clever for them and so a second robber was also put to death.

The Captain now decided to go himself but, wiser than the rest, he did not mark the house, but looked at it so closely that he could not fail to remember it.

He returned, and ordered his men to go into the neighbouring villages and buy nineteen mules and thirty-eight leather jars, all empty, except for one, which was full of oil.

The Captain put one of his men, fully armed, into each jar. Then he rubbed the jars with grease so they looked as if they were full of oil.

Then the nineteen mules were loaded with thirty-seven robbers in jars, and the jar of oil, and they reached the town by dusk. The Captain stopped his mules in front of Ali Baba's house, and said to Ali Baba, who was sitting outside in the cool, "I have carried this oil a long way to sell at tomorrow's market, but it is now so late that I know not where to stay the night, unless you will do me a favour and take me in."

Though Ali Baba had seen the Captain of the robbers in the forest, he did not recognise him in the disguise of an oil merchant. He wished him welcome, opened his gates for the mules to enter, and told Morgiana to prepare a bed and supper for his guest.

He brought the stranger
into his home, and after
they had eaten, Ali Baba
went again to speak to
Morgiana in the kitchen.

Meanwhile the Captain
went to the yard, pretending
to look after his mules, but
really to instruct his men.

Beginning at the first jar and ending at the last, he said to each man, "As soon as I throw some stones from the window of my bedroom, jump out of the jars, and I will be with you in a trice."

He returned to the house, and Morgiana led him to his bedroom. She then asked Abdallah, a slave like herself, to help her make some broth in a pot for their master. But as they set to work, the lamp in the kitchen went out.

"We have no more oil left in the house," said Abdallah, "but there is plenty of oil in those jars outside. Why not go and help yourself?" Morgiana agreed this was a good idea and, taking his oil pot, she went into the yard.

When she got close to the
first jar, she was amazed to
hear a voice from inside
ask her softly, "Is it time?"

Now, any other slave but
Morgiana would have
screamed and run away.
But Morgiana, realising
immediately what was
afoot, answered quietly,
"Not yet, but soon."

Then she visited all the
other jars, one by one.

65

And hearing the same question from each, she gave the same answer until she came to the jar of oil.

Realising that her master had been tricked by the oil merchant into allowing thirty-eight robbers into his house, she filled her oil pot and lit her kitchen lamp. Then she went back to the oil jar and filled her largest pan.

She boiled the oil on her fire then poured enough oil into every jar to stifle and kill the robber inside.

When this brave deed was done she went back to the kitchen, put out the fire and the lamp, and waited to see what would happen.

In a quarter of an hour the Captain of the robbers awoke, got up, and opened the window. As all seemed quiet he threw down some little pebbles which hit the jars. He listened, and as none of his men seemed to stir he grew uneasy, and went down into the yard.

He went to the first jar and said, "Are you asleep?" But when he smelt the hot boiled oil, he knew at once that his plot to murder Ali Baba and his household had been discovered.

The Captain soon found
that all of his gang were
dead and, seeing his oil jar
empty, he guessed how
they had died.

In a fearsome rage, he
broke down the garden
door and, climbing over
several walls, made his
escape. Morgiana heard
and saw all this, and,
rejoicing at her success,
went to bed and fell asleep.

At daybreak Ali Baba arose, and, seeing the oil jars still there, asked what had happened.

Morgiana told him to look in the first jar and see if there was any oil. When he saw that instead of oil there was a man, he started back in terror.

"Have no fear," said Morgiana. "The man cannot harm you for he is dead."

When Ali Baba had recovered somewhat from his astonishment, he asked Morgiana what had become of the oil merchant.

"Merchant!" said Morgiana, "He is no more a merchant than I am!" and she told Ali Baba all that had happened, assuring him that the plot had failed and now there was only one robber left.

At once Ali Baba gave Morgiana her freedom, for he owed her his life. They then buried the robbers in Ali Baba's garden, and sold their mules in the market.

Meanwhile, the Captain returned to his lonely cave. Without his companions to share the wealth, it now seemed a terrible place. He resolved to avenge them by killing Ali Baba.

He disguised himself as a merchant, and went into the town, where he took lodgings at an inn. He visited the cave many

times and carried away
many rich materials and
much fine linen, and set up
a shop opposite that of Ali
Baba's son.

He called himself Cogia Hassan and, as he was both polite and well-dressed, he soon made friends with Ali Baba's son and, through him, with Ali Baba whom he often asked to dinner.

Ali Baba, wishing to return the merchant's kindness, invited him to his own house. He welcomed him with a smile and thanked him for his kindness to his son. When the merchant was about to take his leave Ali Baba stopped him and asked, "Where are you going, sir, in such haste? Will you not stay and sup with me?" The merchant refused, saying that he had a reason and, when Ali Baba asked him what that was, he replied, "It is, sir, that I can eat no food that has salt in it."

"If that is all," said Ali Baba, "let me tell you that there shall be no salt in either the meat or the bread that we eat tonight."

He went to give this order to Morgiana, who was much surprised. "Who is this man," she said, "who eats no salt with his meat?"

"He is an honest man, Morgiana," replied her master, "therefore do as I tell you." But Morgiana was curious to see this strange visitor, so she helped Abdallah carry up the dishes. She saw in a moment that Cogia Hassan was the robber Captain and that he carried a dagger under his coat. "I am not surprised," she said to herself, "that this wicked man, who intends to kill my master, will eat no salt with him. Only friends share salt with their food and he is no friend; but I will soon spoil his scheming."

She sent up the supper with Abdallah, while she prepared the bravest of plans. When the dessert had been served, Cogia Hassan was left alone with

Ali Baba and his son. His evil plot was to make them both drunk and then murder them.

In the meantime Morgiana put on a head-dress like a dancing-girl's, and fastened a belt round her waist, from which hung a dagger with a silver hilt.

"Take your tabor, Abdallah," she said, "and let us go and entertain our master."

So Abdallah obediently
went to find his small
drum and when they
arrived at their master's
door Morgiana made a low
curtsey.

"Come in, Morgiana," said
Ali Baba. "Let Cogia Hassan
see your fine dancing."

Now Cogia Hassan was by no means pleased, for he feared that his chance of killing Ali Baba was gone for the present, but he pretended to be glad to see Morgiana, and Abdallah began to play and Morgiana started to dance.

After she had performed several dances she drew her dagger and made passes with it, sometimes pointing it at herself and sometimes at her guests, as if it were part of the dance. Suddenly, out of breath, she snatched the tabor from Abdallah with her left hand and, holding the dagger in her right, held out the tabor to her master. Ali Baba and his son each put a piece of gold into it, as was the custom.

Cogia Hassan, seeing that she was coming to him, pulled out his purse. But while his hands were busy, Morgiana plunged the dagger into his heart.

"Wretched girl!" cried Ali Baba in astonishment. "Whatever you have done will surely ruin us!"

"I did this to *save* you, master, not to ruin you," answered Morgiana.

"See here," she said, opening the false merchant's coat and showing the dagger that he had been hiding. "See what an enemy you have been entertaining! Look at him! He is both the false oil merchant and the Captain of the Forty Thieves."

Ali Baba was so grateful to Morgiana for thus saving his life that he offered her to his son in marriage, for they had long been in love. And a few days later the wedding was celebrated with great splendour.

After the feasting was over, Ali Baba at last set off for the cave.

"Open, Sesame!" he cried, and the door flew open at

once. In went Ali Baba and saw that all the treasure was still there. He brought away as much gold as he could carry, and returned to town, a rich man.

In time, he told his son the secret of the cave, which his son handed down in his turn, so the children and grandchildren of Ali Baba were rich for the rest of their lives.

Ali Baba and the Forty Thieves belongs to one of the greatest story collections of all time: *The Tales of the Arabian Nights*, also known as *The Book of One Thousand and One Nights*. These stories were first written many hundreds of years ago and include *Aladdin and the Wonderful Lamp*, *The Voyages of Sinbad the Sailor* and *The Magic Carpet*.

They were originally told by the beautiful Princess Scheherezade to the suspicious Prince of Tartary, who had threatened to behead her at daybreak. But her tales were so exciting that, as the sun rose, he longed to hear how they ended and so pardoned her life for one more day, until after one thousand and one nights Scheherezade had won his trust and his heart.